Have You Started Yet?

Written by Ruth Thomson

Illustrated by Jane Eccles

Foreword by Dr. Barbara Zipkin, OB/GYN

Designed by S. Pomeroy

PSS!

PRICE STERN SLOAN

ISBN: 0-8431-7950-3
3 5 7 9 10 8 6 4 2

Library of Congress Cataloging-in-Publication Data
Thomson, Ruth.
  Have you started yet? / Ruth Thomson ; illustrated by Jane Eccles.
    p.   cm.
  Includes bibliographical references.
  Summary: Explains how and why menstrual periods happen, what they
are like, and what to do about them.

  1. Menstruation—Juvenile literature.   [1. Menstruation.]
I. Eccles, Jane, ill. II. Title.
QP263.T47   1996
612.6' 62--dc20   96-18038
                                                      CIP
                                                      AC

For my mother

−R. T.

Acknowledgements

The author would like to thank the three hundred or so girls, boys, and women whose detailed answers to questionnaires and interviews form the backbone of this book. She would also like to thank the following individuals and organizations for their help, advice, constructive criticism, and encouragement: Cynthia Walton; Hazel Slavin; Lynda Measor; Mike Shields, BSc, FRCS, MRCOG; Pam Chrismas; The Kids Book Group (Catherine Brighton, Nicci Crowther, Anita Harper, Ann Heyno, Christine Roche); Bhupinder Sandhu, MBBS, MRCP; Gill Haymer; Ruth Parrish; Judy Bastyra; Barry Scherer; Dr. Ellen Goudsmit; Pippa Cleator; Gail Chester; Jane Jenks; Elinor Williams; Roy Pennington; Miss J. M. Baugh; Catherine McManus; Roger Lawrence; Nicola Ruck; Robinsons of Chesterfield; Mary Abbott of Kotex Products Advisory Service; Tampax; Grapevine; Janice Saunders; Debbie Miller; Joyce Rosser (Deputy Director of the FPA Education Unit); Dilys Went (Lecturer in Human Biology, University of Warwick); Diane Jameson of Smith and Nephew; Coralie Tiffin; Joan Walsh (Health Policy and Research Officer, FPA); Anna and Judith Shipman; Subashini Puvanendrampillai; Alex Hegazy; Ivana Mackinnon; John Coleman (Director of the Trust for the Study of Adolescence); Joanna Coleman; Alys Fowler.

Contents

Contents

Foreword
by Dr. Barbara Zipkin, OB/GYN

Puberty is the time when the body, which has been growing steadily since you were born, suddenly gets ambitious. Hair sprouts, breasts appear, and you bleed every few weeks without being hurt. Puberty can be a weird and scary time if you don't know what it's all about.

Have You Started Yet? explains the changes your body is going through, why it's doing what it's doing, and how to deal with it. You can compare your experiences with those of many other young women who have revealed what it's like to start having a period and to be inside a body which morphs from girl to woman.

This book doesn't blush, stammer, or stare at its feet while it tells you about such subjects as vaginas, cramps, and underarm hair. *Have You Started Yet?* is a manual for you to learn about you. It explains what happens on the outside and on the inside of your body. It tells you what to do when you have your period, and how you may feel when you have your period.

There are pictures that show you what a woman's body looks like, and how to insert a tampon. There is a chart included for you to use to keep track of the emotional and physical changes that occur throughout your menstrual cycle. There are lists of addresses for additional information, should you want to learn more. This book gives you the skinny on it all—it isn't a textbook, and there are no tests—it's simply about your body, your life.

Every young woman's experience of puberty is unique even though the story usually remains pretty much the same. It's that variation that can lead to the worry: "Am I normal?" My puberty worry consisted of The Wait for Breasts; nothing happened fast enough for me. My best friend developed big boobs way too fast for her taste. What are you supposed to do while waiting for breasts or zooming through puberty?

- Throw away your tape measure.
- Exercise. Exercise is always good, even if it won't make your breasts bigger or smaller. Not even that elbows out, fists pumping "We must, we must, we must increase our busts," exercise.
- Listen to loud music.
- Be easy on yourself. Accept your body for what it is and have fun guessing what it will become.

Have You Started Yet? tells you what's normal, and what to do if you're concerned about some aspect of menstruation. Other young women share their stories of worries and rejoicing over their steps to womanhood. There are even note pages in the back to write your personal information on! Everything in this book is designed to help ease the worries and encourage the rejoicing.

Author's Introduction

What's in This Book?

This book is about the changes that girls experience sometime between the ages of nine and seventeen. It is particularly about periods, something that most women in the world have for thirty or more years of their lives. This book will tell you how and why periods happen, what they are like, and what to do about them. It gives practical suggestions for dealing with possible difficulties and answers all sorts of questions people often ask.

Before I wrote this, I sent out hundreds of questionnaires, went to lots of schools and interviewed many women, girls, and boys to discover what their experiences had been like and to find out what they wanted to know about most. I have included a lot of their quotes throughout the book, so that you can see how enormously experiences and attitudes can differ.

Although this book has been written mainly for girls, it is important that boys read it, too. Girls often feel that periods are a secret they must keep from boys, but the more boys know, the better they will understand girls' feelings and the less embarrassed and awkward they may feel themselves.

Don't feel you have to read the book all at once. It's been written for you to use as a reference book, to find out things when you need them. Share it with your friends, and be bold enough to pass it on to a boy!

Interview About Gynecological Exams, with Dr. Barbara Zipkin, OB/GYN

Q: *When should a young woman have her first gynecological exam?*

A: Unless you have had or are experiencing something physically alarming or notably different, you should have your first gynecological exam whenever you become sexually active. If you have not been sexually active and your sexual development has been nothing out of the ordinary, you should see a gynecologist when you are eighteen years old.

Q: *How do most young women feel about their first gynecological exam?*

A: Most people are a little nervous, but they ultimately calm down when we talk first. However, I've had girls freak out with fear about their first gynecological exam: "Will I still be a virgin?" "Will I still be able to get pregnant when I'm older?" You will be unchanged after your gynecological exam. You need to know that a gynecological exam, while important for making sure you are physically okay, is not a big deal, and under regular circumstances does not even take very long.

Q: *Should young women take their mothers with them to their gynecological exam?*

A: Whatever makes you feel most comfortable. Mothers are usually far more nervous than their daughters. Sometimes the girls give me this look which means, "Oh, my mom! You know how mothers are...." It's also more difficult to talk to a girl with her mother there. The girl may worry about what her mother will think instead of giving me an honest answer—especially about any sexual experiences she might have had.

It's natural for mothers to be concerned, but I usually have good news to tell. I'll hear kids whispering to their mothers in the hallway after the exam, "See? I told you it was nothing!"

Q: *What happens when a young woman arrives for her gynecological exam?*

A: When you come to my office for a gynecological exam, you are weighed and your blood pressure is taken. I'll meet you either in the exam room or in my office. A typical conversation usually starts out much like this one:

"What brings you here today?

"A bus."

"How are you feeling?"

"I don't know, you're the doctor."

What I'm trying to find out is the state of your general health and if there are any indications of problems. Remember, your doctor is on your side—and you're not the first nervous teen she's ever seen.

Q: *What questions do you ask?*

A: I ask for a detailed personal and family health history. Questions about family history include information on when relatives reached puberty, if there are serious diseases in the family that affect gynecological health, history of cancers, and any physical defects which might be pertinent. If you are in the office because you suspect a problem, I need to know about it. For example, if your periods are very irregular (such as more than two and a half months apart—irregularity is not uncommon for the first decade or so of a young woman's cycle), I need to know if you have a relative who has had similar symptoms.

I need to know how you're developing physically and in what stage of puberty you are. For that reason, I try to determine if breast development is occurring, if there is underarm and pubic hair, and if menstruation has begun. If you menstruate, I need to know something about your cycle—how often you get your period and what your period is like for you. I also ask when you had your last period.

I ask about any serious illnesses you may have had, injuries, or unusual physical conditions like allergies. I ask if you are on medication or taking some kind of drug—this is important because if I prescribe a medication for you, I need to know what else might be in your system. I need to know if you are sexually active, and if so, what type of birth control you use.

These factors tell me about your physical health and help me to provide a thorough exam.

Q: *What happens next?*

A: When you go into the exam room, my nurse or I give you a paper gown and then leave while you change. You take everything off, put on the gown, and sit on the examining table. The table is not designed for lounging, it has metal stirrups for the patient's feet. The table was also not intended to be a torture table, it's simply that it's designed so the doctor can reach what he or she needs to reach, which means pretty much every part of the patient.

I return to the room and ask you to lie down on your back. "Ooo, nice picture on the ceiling," is what I often hear. I've got a picture of Paul McCartney on the ceiling of the exam room so you have something to look at, focus on, and make you feel less nervous.

Q: *What happens during the exam?*

A: We chat while I perform a breast exam. First, I look at the breasts to determine stage of development. Then I feel the breasts, starting from the outside and moving toward the nipples. I check the breasts for any lumps or bumps. Next I test the nipples for discharge.

I move to the belly, pressing on it looking for any lumps that don't belong, and learning if there are any spots that are tender to the touch. Everyone's ticklish. I'm trying to check them and they're giggling and wiggling. Some people are shy, they can't stop moving one hand here or there or shifting their gown. This is normal.

Q: *What about the pelvic exam?*

A: Most people tell me they hate the pelvic exam. I say, "Which do you hate more, the gynecologist or the dentist? Me? I hate the dentist more." The pelvic exam is not painful. You'll feel pressure on your vagina, belly, and rectum, but that's about it.

You put your feet in the metal stirrups and scoot to the edge of the table. I sit on a stool between the stirrups. At this point, I put on a stern face and say, "I'll be very upset if you kick."

Q: *What happens during a pelvic exam?*

A: The pelvic exam begins with me looking at the outside of the genital area. With plastic gloves on, I touch the outside of the vagina and say, "Relax your muscles and breathe out." Next I slide a speculum inside the vagina. "It's cold," everyone says. A speculum is made of metal or plastic and looks like two spoons put together that separate when I turn a little wheel. For a young girl, I'll use a small nasal speculum. There are sizes appropriate for different ages and amount of sexual activity.

The purpose of the speculum is to allow me to get a look inside the vagina all the way to your cervix. When I open the speculum, there's a little pressure on the rectum, but that's it. I look for anything out of the ordinary: bumps, cuts, or an unusually colored discharge.

Q: *How do you take a pap smear?*

A: The pap smear occurs during the pelvic exam

and is done to check for changes in the cervical cells. The complete results of this test are known a few days after the appointment. I use a cotton swab and a very tiny brush which is about the size of a mascara brush. I take a sample of cells from the cervical opening. This procedure usually feels like a quick, light pinch. The pap smear takes about thirty seconds.

I then carefully remove the speculum. I insert a finger into the vagina or in the case of someone very young, into the rectum. I push up on the cervix, push down on the abdomen and uterus, and gently press the ovaries. With these tests I check the position, shape, contour, and size of the different parts of the body. Then I remove my finger and pull off my gloves.

When people say, "Is that it?"

I answer, "Yeah, unless you want me to do it again."

"That was nothing," is the usual relieved reply.

Q: *What happens after the exam?*

A: I give you a tissue to wipe yourself, tell you everything went well, and ask you to get dressed and meet me in my office. When you come to my office, we discuss the exam. If the appointment has been made because you had noticed a situation which you thought might be something out of the ordinary, we again discuss your reasons for coming to the office and the conclusions I have reached.

We talk about birth control options, prevention of sexually transmitted diseases, and number of sexual partners, if any. There are so many birth control options, the decision really comes down to what you are willing to do and how many partners you have. If you are sexually active I stress safe sex practices. I encourage condom use no matter what, because of sexually transmitted diseases such as AIDS.

We discuss your general health. It's important to eat the right foods and exercise regularly in order to remain healthy.

Q: *What kind of situations would warrant a trip to the gynecologist for a young woman who is not sexually active and is under eighteen?*

A: There are a number of symptoms which would warrant a trip to the gynecologist:

- If a girl does not have her period by age fifteen and also has not developed sexual characteristics such as breasts and hair,

- If she doesn't have her period by age fifteen and has been physically mature for a couple of years,

- If periods are less than twenty-one days from the first day of bleeding to the first day of the next period,

- If she is spotting frequently between periods,

- If her periods are longer than two to two-and-a-half months apart,

- If there are changes that are out of the ordinary, such as suddenly developing a big belly and very bad acne.

Most variations within a normal menstrual cycle do not indicate changes that need medical attention. For example, breast tenderness does change throughout the menstrual cycle. Vaginal discharge changes color, consistency, and amount. Other minor bodily changes are normal and do not warrant a trip to the gynecologist every time they occur. I do encourage patients to call me again, even between visits, if they have any questions or concerns.

Q: *What can a young woman do to make her period more comfortable?*

A: It is normal and common (unfortunately!) to suffer from headaches, cramps, diarrhea, or constipation during a period. The advice I usually give to women who are suffering from painful periods is to use heating pads, nonprescription pain relievers, and anti-inflammatory over-the-counter medications.

Q: *What about PMS?*

A: My advice for troublesome premenstrual syndrome is to avoid drinking caffeine the week before your period starts and to use nonprescription anti-inflammatory medicine. If the problems become suddenly more severe during a period or before its onset, it is best to see a gynecologist.

Q: *Anything else you'd like to say?*

A: The more information a young woman has about her body, the more able she is to take care of it. This book offers good information on puberty and periods—it's a good owner's manual for a young woman's teen body!

I WAS ABOUT ELEVEN. I NOTICED BLOODSPOTS ON MY PAJAMAS JUST AS I WAS GOING TO BED. I WENT DOWNSTAIRS TO TELL MY MOM I HAD STARTED MY PERIOD.

Chapter 1
Talking About Periods

At some point, usually between the ages of nine and seventeen, girls start having periods. The scientific word for them is menstruation (pronounced men-stroo-AY-shun), but people often use slang words instead, such as: time of the month, having the curse, being on the rag, having a period, monthly visitor, Aunt coming to visit.

A girl's first period is a sign that her body is getting ready to be able to conceive a baby. The thing that tells her that her period has started is blood appearing from an opening between her legs, called the *vagina* (to find out what this is, turn to page 45).

Usually blood is a sign that there's something wrong with your body, like a cut or a scrape. But when you have a period, there's *nothing* wrong with your body, and you haven't hurt yourself. In fact, it's the opposite. Your first period shows you that your body is developing and working in a new way, exactly as it's programmed to do.

Starting your period doesn't change you overnight, nor does it mean you have to act differently than you did before. It's just one of many changes that will happen to you as you grow up.

In your great-grandmother's time, periods were considered very hush-hush and secretive; but these days, people are usually much more open about them. The more you know about periods, the better prepared you'll be when they happen to you. Although this book should give you most of the information you need to know, it's a good idea, if you can, to share your ideas and feelings with someone you're close to, such as your mom, an older sister or cousin, your dad, or your grandma, just as these girls did.

A girl at school told me she bled
regularly and had to wear something to
absorb it. She said all girls had it
eventually. I couldn't believe it. I thought she
had some terrible disease and had been told

this story to comfort her. I told my mom what the girl had said and asked if it was true. She said it was and told me all about getting my period.

My sister was really nice to me when I started my period. We didn't used to get along—she is eight years older than I. She gave me a sanitary napkin and showed me how to put it on. That was nice. It felt like I was being cared for.

I NEVER REALLY THOUGHT ABOUT THE CHANGES TO MY BODY. THEY HAPPENED. AND I ACCEPTED THEM.

Chapter 2
What's Happening to My Body?

Up to about the age of eight or nine, girls and boys look very much alike. They have similarly shaped bodies, with no real waist or hips, and slim shoulders. They both have flat chests with small nipples and their voices sound similar. They have the same organs for breathing, moving, and digesting food. As they grow, all their organs grow, too, but they don't change in any way.

Some time after the age of nine, often at eleven or twelve, boys' and girls' bodies start changing. This change is called *puberty*. The changes mean

BEFORE PUBERTY

their bodies are getting ready to have children when they're older. It doesn't mean everyone will automatically or necessarily have children. That choice will be up to them, when they're ready to make it.

At puberty, a tiny gland at the base of the brain, called the *pituitary,* sends chemicals, called *hormones,* into the bloodstream. These reach the sex glands and start them working. In girls, these glands are called *ovaries* and in boys, *testicles.* These glands, in turn, start to produce hormones of their own, which trigger all the sexual changes in the rest of the body. As a result, men and women end up looking different.

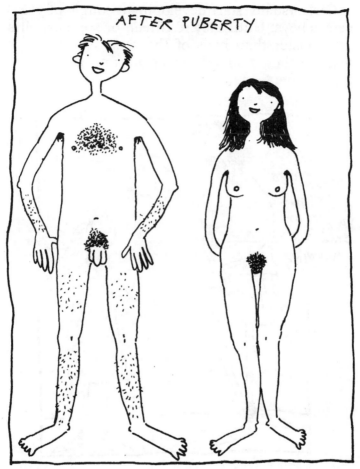

AFTER PUBERTY

   The changes don't happen to everyone at the same time. You might develop sooner or later than your friends, sisters, and brothers. Each person has his or her own built-in body timetable, and grows and changes at his or her own pace. There's nothing you can do to speed it up. Whenever the changes start, by the time you end your teens, they should be completed.

Girls usually start developing a couple of years before boys. Until they're fifteen or so, most girls grow faster than boys of the same age. As boys mature, they gradually catch up and grow taller than many girls.

Before puberty you grow so slowly, year by year, that you probably haven't been aware of growing. At puberty, you'll notice a sudden surge and, as a result, you have to get to know your body all over again. As you become aware of your own body, you'll probably also become more aware of other people's bodies. You may worry that some part of you isn't exactly how you'd like it to be, but just remember that almost everyone else is worrying, too!

I felt round and wanted to be straight.

I was tall, thin, and flat-chested. I longed to grow some curves.

I hated my breasts for being so small.

I was embarrassed that my breasts were larger than the other girls' in my class.

What changes happen to boys?

Boys grow taller and stronger and their feet grow bigger. Their shoulders broaden, their chest widens, and muscles start to develop. The *penis* and *testicles* (the male sex organs) start to grow bigger and pubic hair starts sprouting. The testicles start producing *sperm* (the male seeds). Often, the skin around the testicles may redden and coarsen.

As boys continue to grow, their vocal chords grow. This eventually makes their voices deeper, although they may squeak from time to time at first. Hair starts growing under their arms, on their faces, and perhaps on their chests as well. The hair on their arms and legs grows thicker and darker and their pubic hair becomes thick and curly. Their skin gets oiler and their sweat glands become more active.

What changes happen to girls?

Girls grow taller and heavier. Their faces become fuller, their hips become wider and rounder, their breasts start to develop, and pubic hair starts to appear. Their sex organs start to change.

As they become more mature, girls start having periods, their breasts fill out, underarm hair starts appearing, their sweat glands become active, and their skin gets oilier.

All about breasts

Growing breasts is one of the first changes you're likely to notice. The nipples become larger, darker, and more prominent. They may become very sensitive to touch. Breasts develop gradually. Some girls notice a tingling feeling or occasional soreness. This is normal and has to do with the growth of breasts.

Breasts, like other parts of the body, come in all shapes and sizes. There's no such thing as perfect breasts, even if magazines and advertisements try to persuade you otherwise. If your mother and female relatives (on either your mother's or father's side) have small or large breasts, the chances are that your breasts will end up a similar size.

If you have small breasts and have had your period for a few years, your breasts are unlikely to grow much bigger. If you've only just started your period, or not started yet, and your breasts are growing, you can expect them to grow some more.

Breasts don't always grow evenly. Sometimes one grows faster than the other. Don't worry about it—they will even out in time. It's unlikely, however, that they will ever match up exactly. Your hands and the sides of your face don't match up exactly, either!

Girls are often concerned about growing breasts—what's a pleasure for one, is agony for another. . . .

I felt very proud. I measured their growth regularly and really looked forward to wearing a bra.

I HAD BREASTS AT TEN AND WAS AMAZED HOW JEALOUS SOME GIRLS WERE IF THEY DIDN'T HAVE BREASTS AS LARGE AS THE NEXT GIRL'S. WE ALL COMPARED SHAPES AND SIZES.

I WAS COMPLETELY
FLAT-CHESTED UNTIL I WAS
15. I THOUGHT I'D NEVER
GROW BREASTS AT ALL.

I didn't really like my breasts growing.
I knew I'd have to wear a bra and I felt
embarrassed.

Girls who develop early sometimes feel self-con-
scious, while girls who develop later might feel left
out. But whatever size your breasts end up, there's
not much point in worrying about how you
measure up with anyone else. You're stuck with
them, so you should try and accept them, however hard that might seem at first.

It was uncomfortable at first to have a small bust compared with others'. But now I've come to realize that a small bust runs in my family.

Your sex organs

As well as your changing size and shape, parts of you develop in new ways. For instance, your external sex organs, known as the *vulva,* become larger and more sensitive. If you've never had a close look at your vulva before, it's worth spending a moment getting to know what it's like. Then you can see how it changes through puberty. The more you get to know and value your body, the better you'll feel about it. You'll also find it useful if you want to try using tampons during your period (see page 64).

Make sure you're not in a rush and have some privacy and clean hands. You'll need a mirror and a good light. Sit on the floor or a bed, with your legs apart and your knees bent. Hold the mirror up between your legs and prop this book where you can see it easily. See if you can identify everything from the picture on the next page. Remember though, girls' vulvas differ as much as every other part of their bodies, so your vulva might not look exactly like this one. Your lips might be bigger or smaller or you may not have a hymen.

➼ **The mons** is a fatty pad which protects the pubic bone. It becomes covered with pubic hair.

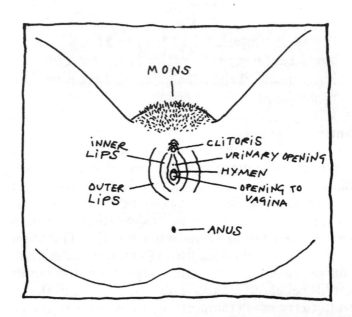

••◆ The outer lips are folds of fatty tissue that protect the inner area and keep it moist and healthy. They become covered with pubic hair on the outside. During puberty, they gradually become larger, darker, fleshier, and sensitive to touch.

••◆ The inner lips are the folds of tissue you will see if you gently part the outer lips. They are hairless, moist, and may be pink or brown. Usually they lie together and protect the opening. You may have inner lips that stick out beyond the outer ones, one lip longer than the other, or very small ones.

All of these variations are normal. At the top of the lips, the folds join together and cover the clitoris.

The clitoris is the most sensitive part of your vulva. You'll only be able to see its tip, a bump about the size of a pea. The rest is hidden under the inner lips. If you can't find the clitoris, gently press around where you think it should be. When you notice a pleasant sensation, you've probably found it.

The urinary opening (also known as the *urethra*) is a tiny hole just below the clitoris, where your pee comes out.

The opening to the vagina is the bigger opening below the urethra. It looks small, but can stretch a great deal. It leads to the uterus (womb) inside your body.

The hymen is a thin, stretchy fold of skin that may partly cover the opening to the vagina. Usually there are one or more openings in it through which blood can flow during a period. In the past, people thought they could tell a girl was a virgin if her hymen was unbroken. In fact, many girls are born without a hymen. A girl's hymen is often stretched or broken quite naturally by exercise such as jumping or riding a bike. Virginity has nothing to do with whether or not you have a hymen. You stop being a virgin only when you have sexual intercourse.

The anus is the opening through which solid waste comes out of your body. It is not part of your sex organs.

Pubic and body hair
When your pubic hair first starts growing, it is soft and colorless. Eventually it darkens and coarsens. It is usually darker than the hair on your head, or may be a different color altogether. Some girls have very thick pubic hair, others have only a small amount.

Hair will also start growing under your arms and on your arms and legs. It is not uncommon for girls to find hair growing around their nipples and across their tummies as well.

I USED TO THINK THAT PERIODS WERE JUST SOMETHING EXTERNAL THAT HAPPENED. NOW I REALIZE THAT THEY'RE PART OF ALL THE OTHER CHANGES THAT ARE TAKING PLACE.

Chapter 3

What's Happening Inside My Body?

All about your reproductive organs

In addition to all the changes you can see happening, other important changes—ones you can't see—are happening inside your body at the same time. The reproductive organs that you were born with start to grow and develop.

Each one is designed to play a part in producing a new life—whether or not they ever actually do so.

The reproductive organs are well protected inside your body. To find out precisely where they are, put your index fingers on the bone just above where your legs meet.

Now put your thumbs on the front of your hip bones. Your reproductive organs are enclosed inside this area. They are a similar size for everyone regardless of body size.

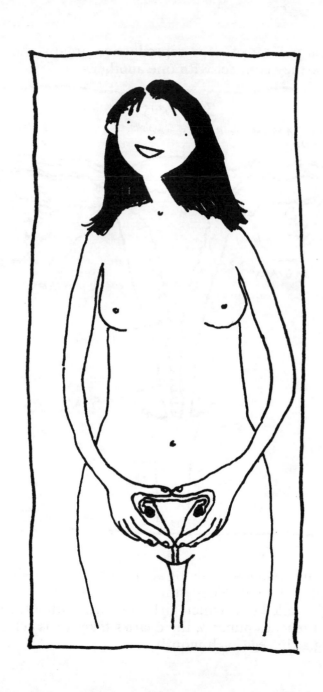

This picture of your reproductive organs shows how they connect with one another.

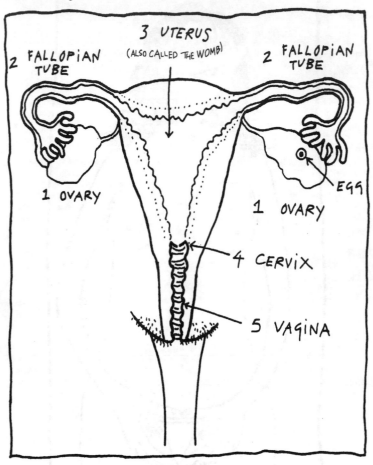

1 The ovaries are both about the size and shape of an almond. They store thousands of tiny egg cells called *ova*, which girls are born with. Once a girl reaches puberty, the ovaries take turns releasing a ripe egg each month.

2 The fallopian tubes are both about the length and thickness of a ballpoint pen. One end, fringed and shaped like a funnel, is partly wrapped around an ovary. The other end opens out into the uterus.

When an egg comes out of an ovary, the fringes of the tube catch it and draw it into the tube. The egg then travels through the tube toward the uterus.

3 The uterus (also called the womb) is a hollow, stretchy organ, shaped like an upside-down pear. It has strong walls of muscle and is lined with glands and blood vessels. It starts growing bigger when you're about ten and by the time you are eighteen, it will be the size of a clenched fist. When a woman is pregnant, this is where the unborn baby grows. During pregnancy, the uterus grows to the size of a volleyball—but goes back to its normal size after the birth.

4 The cervix is the entrance to the uterus. It usually stays closed. It opens slightly during a period to let the menstrual blood trickle out, and only fully when a baby is born.

5 The vagina is the passageway from the uterus to the outside of the body. It is where the flow of blood comes out during a period. It is also where a penis will enter during heterosexual intercourse. The vagina is also known as the *birth canal*. Its walls of soft, folded skin stretch very easily to allow a baby to be born.

The life of an egg

Once you start having periods, this is what happens inside your body every month.

Menstrual cycle ends

Approximate time of ovulation

The Menstrual Cycle

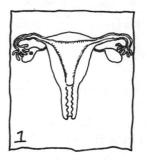

1 At about the time your period stops, a tiny egg cell starts to ripen in one of the ovaries. The next month, an egg cell will ripen in the other ovary.

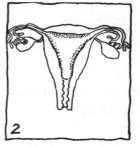

2 The ovary sends a hormone signal to the uterus. The lining of the uterus begins to thicken. About fourteen days after your last period, the ripe egg bursts out of the ovary. This is called *ovulation*.

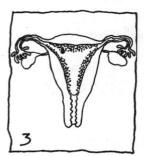

3 The egg travels down a fallopian tube toward the uterus. By now the lining of the uterus has become thick and spongy to make a soft bed for the egg if it becomes fertilized. But the *only* way an egg can become fertilized is if it joins with a sperm.

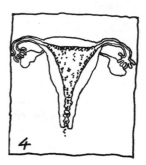

4 If the egg is *not* fertilized, the spongy lining breaks down. The blood vessels contract, causing bleeding. The lining and the remains of the egg flow out of the uterus and through your vagina. This is known as your period.

What will my first period feel like?

There's no one answer to this question. It varies from girl to girl. There is one sign that many girls notice, which often means their periods will soon start. This is how one girl describes it:

Six months before I started, I sometimes got a creamy white discharge which stained my panties.

Vaginal discharge is a normal and healthy sign that the sex hormones are becoming active.

Like any other first experience, you'll probably always remember your first period. Feelings about it differ widely. Some girls feel excited because it's something they've been looking forward to.

I had my first period when I was eleven. I was watching TV in my nightie. When I got up to go to bed, there was blood on the nightie. My sister, age ten, said, "You lucky thing, you've started your period!" I went upstairs and put on a sanitary napkin (which I'd practiced doing before). I told everyone who would listen. I felt very proud.

For other girls it can be a terrible shock, particularly if no one has told them about periods. They think they must have hurt themselves or become sick.

I WOKE UP ONE MORNING TO FIND BLOOD ON THE SHEETS. IT REALLY SCARED ME BECAUSE I DIDN'T KNOW WHERE IT CAME FROM. I THOUGHT I WAS BLEEDING TO DEATH INSIDE. I DIDN'T KNOW IT WAS A PERIOD. NO ONE HAD TOLD ME ABOUT THEM.

Sometimes, even if a girl knows about periods, her first one comes as a surprise, without any warning.

I went to the toilet and there it was—blood on my panties.

I woke up one morning, and there was blood on my bed.

Quite a few girls do have a warning that something is happening—even if they don't know what it is.

49

One night I had strange cramps and couldn't sleep. When I got up the next morning, I went to the bathroom and found blood.

I had an ache low down in my tummy and felt tired, and then my period started.

I felt uncomfortable and as if I wanted to pee all the time. I didn't feel sick, but I did not feel well. Then I discovered my period had started.

No one's first period is exactly the same. When your first period happens, it might be long or short, painful or painless, and the flow may be red, rusty, or brown. See how these girls' experiences differed.

It was very, very dark brown and very smooth and very thick.

It wasn't red like real blood. It only lasted a day or two.

I bled for two whole weeks. I couldn't believe it.

I was surprised that it didn't hurt and by the way the blood came out little by little and didn't pour out as I had expected.

I had bad stomachaches in P.E., but I didn't notice any blood until I got home. It was a kind of rusty color.

What do I need to do when I start?

The most important thing to remember is that periods happen to almost every single girl and woman, and that there's no need to panic or to feel shy about asking for help. Most women will be very sympathetic and do their best to help you. Periods can start at any time and not necessarily when you're best prepared for them. You're most likely to notice you've started when you're in the bathroom and see bloodstains on your underwear. If you're at home, your mom, sister, or grandma can show you what to do. If you're at school, ask the school nurse, a teacher, or a friend for help.

I went to the bathroom and there was some blood. I yelled for my mom and she showed me how to use a pad.

I started in the swimming pool at school. I had a stomachache and could see blood coming out of me. I got out and told the man teacher I was going to the bathroom. I saw a woman teacher and told her I'd started. She gave me a pad.

If you're somewhere where you feel it's impossible to ask for help, you can always make do (see page 74). But if you can talk to someone, you'll avoid having experiences like these.

I was staying with a friend. In the morning I found blood when I went to the bathroom. I knew what it was, but I didn't know what to do. I had no sanitary napkins or anything, and I was too shy to ask or tell anyone. I stuffed toilet paper in my underpants and hoped that all my layers of clothes would keep the blood hidden. It was a miserable day. I couldn't relax or think of anything else.

I got a sanitary napkin out of a machine in the school bathroom. It was folded in a square. I didn't know how to put it on. So I put it in my underpants just as it was—in a small square. When I got home, Mom showed me what to do.

What's a normal period?

There's no such thing! The only thing that's certain is that periods start and stop by themselves. Some may last two days, some may last eight days. Some people have periods every twenty-one days and some people have them every thirty-five days. Most people have them somewhere in between. Sometimes periods are heavy, sometimes they're light. Sometimes the flow may be heaviest for the first two days and then taper off and sometimes it might be exactly the opposite. The color of the flow may change, too. It often starts rusty red, becomes bright red when the flow is fastest, and then turns brownish by the end.

How often will I get my period?

For the first two years after your period starts, there will probably be no regular pattern to them. It's quite OK to have a period once every three, four, five, or even every six weeks, or to have a period one month and not the next.

After a couple of years, as your hormones settle down, you should begin to notice a more regular pattern to your periods. If you're worried that you don't have a regular pattern, see page 106 for more information about irregular and interrupted periods. You might also like to keep a record of your cycle by using the calendar on pages 78–79.

I USE PADS BECAUSE IT'S EASY TO KNOW WHEN TO CHANGE THEM...

PADS

I USE TAMPONS BECAUSE THEY'RE HIDDEN AWAY AND NO ONE CAN TELL WHEN I HAVE MY PERIOD. NO MATTER WHAT I'M WEARING....

Chapter 4

Pads and Tampons

O nce you start having your period, you'll need to wear something to catch the flow of blood. The flow is usually a slow trickle with an occasional spurt. You can't control it. Unlike peeing, a period happens on its own and continues day and night. To avoid staining your clothes, you can use either sanitary napkins (also known as *pads*) or tampons.

Napkins

Sanitary napkins are soft, absorbent pads that you put inside your underpants. They have a leak-proof plastic backing with a sticky strip so you can press them firmly in place on your underpants.

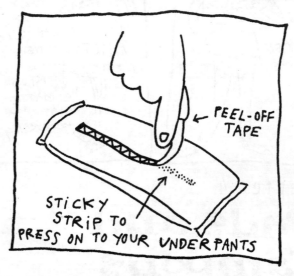

Pads come in different sizes and shapes. You might like to try out several kinds to see which ones you like using the best. Some manufacturers will send samples if you write to them, so you can try out several brands and see which suit you best. Their addresses are on pages 113–115.

Panty liners are the thinnest. You might like to use these on the day you expect your period to start or at the end of your period when the flow is very light.

Standard pads come in several lengths and thicknesses. You will probably find that slim or regular ones give you enough protection. Super pads are generally for women who have a very heavy flow. Longer nighttime pads may be useful to protect your pajamas and sheets when you lie down.

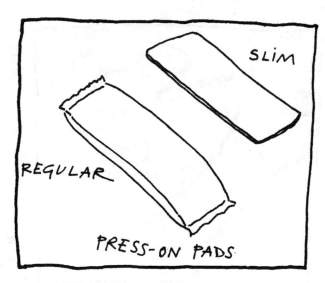

Shaped pads are wider at the front than at the back and have extra padding in the middle. The ends are thin and rounded to make them less bulky.

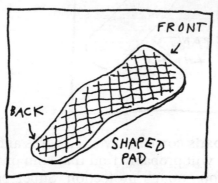

FRONT

BACK

SHAPED PAD

Winged pads have sticky "wings" which fold under the underpants and stick there to stop the pad from moving.

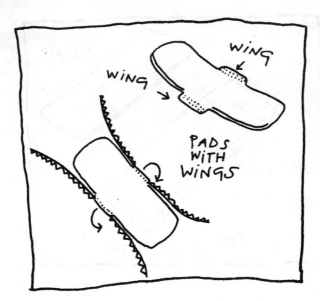

WING

WING

PADS WITH WINGS

Buying pads

You can buy pads at pharmacies, supermarkets, and many convenience stores. They come either loose in boxes, or individually wrapped which can be easier to carry around.

Changing your pad

For the first few days of your period, it's best to change your pad every few hours. This will help prevent stains, funky smells, and any risk of infection. It's easiest to change them in the bathroom. Remember to wash your hands before and after.

Getting rid of used pads

Look at the instructions on the package to find out what you have to do with the kind of pads you use. Some sanitary napkins come with individual wrappers; you simply put on the new one, fold the used one into the wrapper, and toss in the trash. Otherwise, simply fold up the used pad and wrap it in some toilet paper or a bag, then throw it away.

Ask your mom how she would prefer you to get rid of pads and tampons at home. If in doubt when you are out or spending the night away from home, throw away used pads and tampons, don't flush them.

There are often notices in bathrooms in schools, theaters, and other public places that ask you not to flush any type of pad or tampon. Public bathrooms often provide paper or plastic bags and trash cans for sanitary pads and tampons. If a small trash can is not available inside the stall, don't worry, every female your age or older in the bathroom will not think twice if they see you disposing properly of your used pad. It is rude, unsanitary, and unacceptable to simply leave a used pad on the stall floor.

Tampons

A tampon is a tight roll of cotton fibers with a cord attached to one end. You push it into your vagina and leave it there to soak up the period flow *inside* your body. It expands gently, both in length and width inside the vagina, but you should not be able to feel it at all.

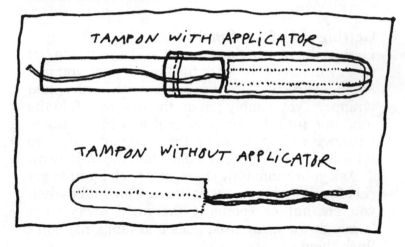

There are two kinds of tampons—those with cardboard or plastic applicators, which help you guide the tampon into place, and those without applicators, which you push in place with your fingers.

Tampons come in several sizes: slender (designed for very petite girls), regular, and super. It's important to use the lowest absorbency tampon for your flow when you begin to menstruate. Start with slender tampons. If they become fully absorbed in *less* than four hours, you need to use regular or super ones instead. But if you take out a regular or super tampon after a few hours and there is a lot of white showing, use slender ones instead.

When to use tampons

There's no set age for starting to use tampons. It's up to you to decide when you're ready. Some girls may find it difficult to insert a tampon at first and may prefer to use pads until they've gotten used to having regular periods.

Some parents might have strong feelings about girls using tampons, and this may be a touchy subject. If you want to try using tampons and your parents don't want to discuss it, talk to your friends. See if they use tampons, and find out what they think of them.

I bought a package of tampons to try. I could not get the hang of them. I asked my mom for advice. She said I was too young to use them. A few months later, I went to stay with a friend, who suggested that we go swimming. I said I had my period and couldn't. My friend used slender tampons. She asked her mom if it would be OK if I used them. She said, "Yes, of course, they're completely harmless." This surprised me after my mom's reaction. Anyway, I tried them, and I've used them ever since.

Discovering your vagina

If you have a problem putting in your first tampon, it's probably because you don't know your body well enough.

The main problem was that I didn't really know where my vagina was, so I didn't know where the tampon went.

I had an idea that my vagina was very narrow and that anything going in or coming out would hurt—happily I discovered that the opposite is true.

If you want to use tampons, it's a good idea to get a feel of what your vagina is like first. Do this when you are relaxed and have a quiet moment on your own, perhaps after a warm bath. **Wash your hands** before parting the lips of your vulva and putting a finger or two inside your vagina. Feel which direction the vagina goes in. Can you feel that it goes at an angle, more toward your back than straight up? This is the angle to aim for when you put in a tampon. Feel the muscles of the vagina walls. These hold the tampon securely in place.

Putting in a tampon

When you decide you're ready to try putting in a tampon, make sure you're relaxed and have plenty of time and privacy. If you're tense and in a hurry, your muscles will tighten up! The best time to try is actually *during* a period, not between periods. You may find it easiest of all during the first two days of a period when the flow is usually heaviest. It's far easier to slide a tampon into a moist vagina than into a dry one. If you find you can't get the tampon in, don't worry. Wait a month or so and then try again until you succeed.

I was really scared and didn't push them high enough at first. Now they're OK.

I think I pushed the tampons in too gently at first. I became frustrated when they didn't magically fit into place. It took quite a while before I got the hang of it. It took me six months before my muscles stopped tensing around them. Now I'm fine with them.

Every package of tampons contains a leaflet that explains exactly how to put them in. Read it carefully before you try. The instructions may seem complicated at first. Once you get used to putting in a tampon, you will be able to do it in a few seconds.

Read the instructions on the following pages so you can learn how to use a tampon.

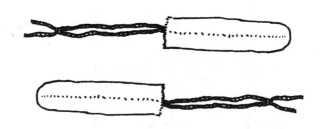

How to use a tampon without an applicator

1 Wash your hands. Unwrap the tear strip and the cellophane wrapper. Gently pull the cord to make sure it is firmly in place. Check that the ends are tied together. If you drop the tampon on the floor by mistake, don't use it!

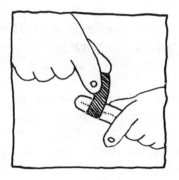

2 Flare out the cord end of the tampon, making a little dimple to put your index finger in.

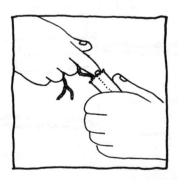

3 Put one foot up on the toilet seat, bathtub, or chair. Breathe deeply and relax. Gently push the tampon with your finger as far into the vagina as it will go. Make sure the cord hangs outside your body.

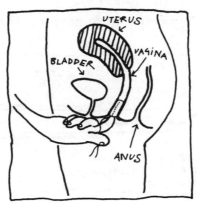

4 If the tampon is in the right place, you shouldn't be able to feel it. If you can feel it, it probably isn't in far enough. The muscles in your vagina hold it in place, so it can't fall out.

To remove it, gently pull on the cord at the same angle as when you put it in. The tampon will slide out and you can dispose of it.

How to use a tampon with an applicator

Some tampons have a pair of tubes that fit together sort of like a telescope. These tubes make up the *applicator.* They help you to position the tampon.

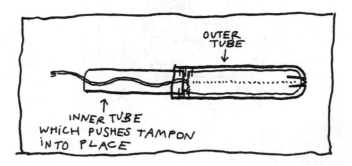

1 Wash your hands. Unwrap a tampon. Make sure the cord dangles from the smaller tube. Stand with one foot raised or crouch with your knees apart. Hold the larger tube (that contains the tampon) at the grooves. With your other hand spread apart the lips of your vulva.

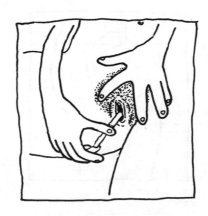

2 Push the outer tube gently into your vagina. Point it toward the small of your back. Don't force it in farther than it will easily go. Push it until most of the outer tube is in your vagina.

3 Keep holding the outer tube. Put your index fin-

ger over the end of the inner tube to hold the cord in place. Push the inner tube completely into the outer tube, so the ends are level. This pushes the tampon out of the tube and into the vagina.

4 Let go of the cord. Remove both tubes and flush them down the toilet or put them in a trash can. Check that the cord hangs freely outside your body.

When you need to change the tampon, gently pull the cord to remove it at the same angle as when you put it in. You can flush or throw it away.

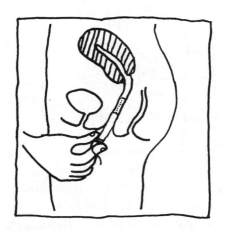

Changing tampons

You need to change a tampon every few hours or so, especially for the first few days of your period when the flow is usually the heaviest. You can tell when a tampon needs changing, because you will notice a kind of bubbling feeling at the base of your vagina or you will see that the cord is blood-stained. Always use a fresh tampon before you go to bed and when you get up. Never leave one in for more than eight hours because you put your body at risk of infection when you leave in a tampon for too long.

Make absolutely sure that you've removed a used tampon before you put in a new one, and don't forget to take out the last tampon of a period. If you notice a strange smell even though you've washed thoroughly, check to see whether you've left in a tampon.

If you have a heavy flow, you might want to use a pad as well as a tampon, particularly at night. If the tampon cannot absorb any more blood, the pad will absorb any leakage.

Facts about tampons

•• Tampons shouldn't be painful to put in. If it hurts when you put one in, it's probably because you haven't aimed it at the right angle. Don't worry about stretching your vagina. The vagina is very elastic—remember, it can stretch wide enough to let a baby's head come through.

•• Tampons can't get lost inside you. The opening to the uterus is so tiny that it is impossible for a tampon to go through it. A tampon will always stay in the vagina. There is *nowhere* else for it to go (see the picture on page 44).

•• Once a tampon is in place, you should not be able to feel it at all. If you can, you haven't pushed it in far enough. Try pushing it in further with your finger, or pull it out and try again with a new one.

•• If, by mistake, you push the cord up into your vagina, you can still pull out the tampon. Wash your hands. Squat down and put your first two fingers into your vagina. Breathe slowly and try to relax. If you can't reach the tampon, try straining hard, as if you were going to the bathroom. Then you should be able to grasp it. If you still can't reach it, try again in the bath or ask someone to help you. Doctors are used to taking out tampons.

➡ A very rare infection, called *toxic shock syndrome*, has been linked with using tampons. It starts like the flu—the symptoms are a sudden high temperature of 102°F (39°C) or more, sickness and diarrhea, a sore throat, dizziness, and a rash that looks like sunburn. If you get any of these symptoms while you're using a tampon, take it out immediately and call the doctor.

Which to use?

Both pads and tampons have their advantages and disadvantages. You'll need to try both to discover which you find easier and more comfortable to use. Here's what several girls say about them.

AT NIGHT I WEAR A PAD. IT'S MORE COMFORTABLE AND GIVES BETTER PROTECTION. IN THE DAY I WEAR TAMPONS.

Advantages

Pads

They're discreet, secure, and I feel confident wearing them.

They are comfortable and easy enough to throw away. I don't think I'd like to try tampons yet. They frighten me a little, but I don't know why.

They are easy to get rid of, and you know when to change them.

TAMPONS ARE CLEAN AND EASY AND DON'T TAKE UP TOO MUCH SPACE IN A BAG. THEY'RE EASY TO PACK WHEN I GO AWAY SOMEWHERE.

Tampons

Using tampons makes a period easier. They're invisible. There's no worrying about smells or disposal. They make me feel more comfortable and relaxed.

I like tampons because they get rid of that messy feeling, but I think they're expensive.

Disadvantages

Pads

They're bulky and awful. They make me shudder.

I always worry about the smell if I can't change them often enough.

They sometimes slip out of place and rub the tops of my thighs.

THEY'RE ALWAYS THERE AND YOU CAN'T FORGET THEM. YOU CAN'T GO SWIMMING OR ANYTHING LIKE THAT.

Tampons

I can't always control my bladder with a tampon in, and I find it hard to put them in when my flow is light.

For the first two days a tampon isn't enough for nighttime. I use a pad as well.

Sometimes I get the angle wrong when I'm putting one in. It kind of bends over and becomes uncomfortable—so I have to replace it with another.

I FIND IT DIFFICULT TO TELL WHEN TO CHANGE THEM—SOMETIMES I FEEL THEM LEAKING AND THEN IT'S TOO LATE.

You might find it interesting to compare the advertisements for different kinds of pads and tampons to see which advantages each one claims.

Sometimes ads play on people's fears of things showing, bad smells, or leaking. If you change whatever you use fairly often, especially during the first two days of a period, you shouldn't need to worry about any of those things.

Be prepared
Make a note in your diary or calendar of the first day of your period, so you know roughly when the next one will happen. Around that time, it's a good idea to carry a pad or a tampon with you when you're out or at school. You may even prefer to wear a panty liner, in case your period starts when you're nowhere near a bathroom.

Sometimes your period may start when you least expect it. If you have nothing with you, you can always use tissues, folded sheets of toilet paper, or a clean handkerchief. Use them just like you would use a sanitary napkin. If your periods are very irregular, or if it would help you feel more prepared, you could always keep a spare pad or tampon in your backpack or in your locker. Even if you don't need the pad or tampon, you may find it comes in handy for one of your friends. An extra pair of underwear is also useful.

Don't feel embarrassed to ask other girls or women if they have an extra pad or tampon you can use. They all have periods, too, so they'll be sympathetic. If you start at school, either the nurse's office or the girl's gym is usually the place to go for supplies. Some schools and public bathrooms have machines where you can buy individual pads or tampons.

...IF YOU DON'T NEED THE PAD OR TAMPON YOU MAY FIND IT COMES IN HANDY FOR ONE OF YOUR FRIENDS.

I NEVER REALLY THOUGHT ABOUT A CYCLE. BUT I SEE MY PERIOD AS A SIGN THAT MY BODY IS WORKING AS IT SHOULD BE.

I LIKE TO CHECK ON THE TIME: I FEEL THAT IF I DIDN'T HAVE PERIODS, TIME WOULD JUST DRIFT ON UNNOTICED.

Chapter 5

You and Your Cycle

Periods are only one part of the menstrual cycle. Since they're the part that seems most noticeable, people often don't bother to think about what's happening to them during the rest of their cycle.

Perhaps you've noticed that on some days you feel great, have loads of energy, and your skin and hair look good. On other days, you feel awful— you can't concentrate properly, you are grumpy with your parents and friends, feel depressed about your looks, and cry more easily.

Sometimes, of course, there is another reason for how you feel. Maybe you've had a celebration or a disappointment, or perhaps you've been complimented or criticized. But sometimes you can't see any reason at all for your feelings. You're not crazy! There is one! It's all to do with your menstrual cycle.

Chart the length of your cycle

January

1	2	3	4	5	6	7
8	9	10	11	12	13	14
15	16	17	18	19	20	21
22	23	24	25	26	27	28
29	30	31				

February

1	2	3	4	5	6	7
8	9	10	11	12	13	14
15	16	17	18	19	20	21
22	23	24	25	26	27	28
(29)						

March

1	2	3	4	5	6	7
8	9	10	11	12	13	14
15	16	17	18	19	20	21
22	23	24	25	26	27	28
29	30	31				

April

1	2	3	4	5	6	7
8	9	10	11	12	13	14
15	16	17	18	19	20	21
22	23	24	25	26	27	28
29	30					

May

1	2	3	4	5	6	7
8	9	10	11	12	13	14
15	16	17	18	19	20	21
22	23	24	25	26	27	28
29	30	31				

June

1	2	3	4	5	6	7
8	9	10	11	12	13	14
15	16	17	18	19	20	21
22	23	24	25	26	27	28
29	30					

The length of your cycle is the number of days between the start of one period and the next. It may be as short as twenty-one days, as long as thirty-five days, or anything in between. All are quite normal. When you first start your period, your cycle is quite likely to be *very* irregular. Use this calendar to help you chart your own cycle. Circle the day you start a period and cross through each day it lasts.

July

1	2	3	4	5	6	7
8	9	10	11	12	13	14
15	16	17	18	19	20	21
22	23	24	25	26	27	28
29	30	31				

August

1	2	3	4	5	6	7
8	9	10	11	12	13	14
15	16	17	18	19	20	21
22	23	24	25	26	27	28
29	30	31				

September

1	2	3	4	5	6	7
8	9	10	11	12	13	14
15	16	17	18	19	20	21
22	23	24	25	26	27	28
29	30					

October

1	2	3	4	5	6	7
8	9	10	11	12	13	14
15	16	17	18	19	20	21
22	23	24	25	26	27	28
29	30	31				

November

1	2	3	4	5	6	7
8	9	10	11	12	13	14
15	16	17	18	19	20	21
22	23	24	25	26	27	28
29	30					

December

1	2	3	4	5	6	7
8	9	10	11	12	13	14
15	16	17	18	19	20	21
22	23	24	25	26	27	28
29	30	31				

Personal Mood Chart

Keep a chart of your feelings

Find out whether and how your cycle affects you by keeping a chart of your feelings. After three or four months, you should be able to see whether any particular feelings arise again and again at the same intervals. Even if you haven't started your period yet, you may still be able to see a pattern.

Filling in your chart

➤ Mark each day of your period with a **P**.
➤ Mark days when your flow is heavier with an **H**.
➤ With your own symbols, pictures, or words, note the days when you feel particularly good or bad.
➤ Weigh yourself the week before and after a period to see if there is any noticeable difference.

MONTH ONE
1
2
3
4
5
6
7
8
9
10
11
12
13
14
15
16
17
18
19
20
21
22
23
24
25
26
27
28
29
30
31

Month Two		Month Three	
1		1	
2		2	
3		3	
4		4	
5		5	
6		6	
7		7	
8		8	
9		9	
10		10	
11		11	
12		12	
13		13	
14		14	
15		15	
16		16	
17		17	
18		18	
19		19	
20		20	
21		21	
22		22	
23		23	
24		24	
25		25	
26		26	
27		27	
28		28	
29		29	
30		30	
31		31	

Everybody is different

No one's cycle is exactly the same. You might find that you have no noticeable pattern at all.

I don't notice any changes in mood due to my period. I'm very moody anyway, and my moods change from hour to hour and day to day without any reason that I can see.

My moods are more affected by whether I have a good or bad day at school and have a good or bad social life than by my period.

On the other hand, you might feel OK most of the time *except* around the time of your period.

Sometimes my nipples hurt the day before a period. I get constipated for the first few days, and I get really bad cramps.

I feel like I can't do much when I have my period, and that makes me annoyed.

OUCH!

I'M SORTA CLUMSY DURING MY PERIOD. I SEEM TO GET A LOT OF CUTS AND SCRATCHES ON MY HANDS...

You may notice that your moods change drastically at different times of the month.

I feel very high after a period, then, just when I think I'm going to do great things in the few weeks following my period, I get low. Now that I know what it is, I try to plan for it.

Or you might feel good for most of your cycle except for the week or so before your period is due. Then you might notice changes to your body.

I can't stand to be touched.

My hair gets greasier more quickly and so does my skin.

MY STOMACH FEELS BLOATED. I GET STOMACH AND BACK ACHES...

My breasts swell and my tummy feels tender. I feel heavy and overweight and get pimples.

Your moods may change at the same time.

I'm miserable and more quiet a week before my period.

I feel stupid and slow.

I feel grumpy and uncomfortable, and I cry easily.

I'm impatient and snarl at people for no reason.

Helpful suggestions

The body and mood changes that happen before a period are called *PMS*, which is short for Pre-Menstrual Syndrome. No one knows for certain why these changes happen, but they're very common. If they bother you, some of the following suggestions may help.

I feel bloated and fat when I've got a period.

If you put on a few pounds when you've got a period, you are probably retaining extra water. Cut down on salty foods, which make the body retain water, and don't drink caffeinated drinks, such as coffee, tea, or soft drinks.

I get crabby and can't seem to help it.

If you get grumpy, irritable, or panicky for no other reason or suddenly feel weak, particularly in the week before a period, these feelings may be made worse when you haven't eaten for a long time. If so, eat snacks at short intervals throughout the day, in addition to your usual meals, to give you extra energy.

I feel like a slug, slow and sleepy.

If you feel especially tired or lazy, try to get some extra rest and sleep in the two weeks before your period is due. It may also help to eat plenty of fruits and vegetables, whole wheat bread, nuts, and seeds. If you have sweet cravings, eat peanuts

or peanut butter and ripe bananas instead, and drink fresh orange juice, herbal teas, and lots of water, rather than binging on cookies or candy.

I put off anything that can possibly be left until after my period.

I SAVE UP NICE THINGS TO DO FOR DAYS WHEN I FEEL DOWN — A GOOD BOOK, KNITTING, MAKING THINGS, LISTENING TO MY FAVORITE MUSIC . . . .

If you keep a chart of how you feel, you can figure out the days when you might feel a little down. Then you can prepare for them and not make plans for too many social events during that time. You may also find that once you know *why* you're feeling a certain way, you can cope better with those feelings anyway.

If none of these suggestions help, it's worth going to see your doctor. Take your chart with you. It will help the doctor see how your symptoms relate to your cycle.

Chapter 6
Be Nice to Yourself

As you grow up, the hormones that cause your period to start also affect other parts of your body, as well as your moods, your appetite, and your energy level. You'll need to start looking after yourself in ways you never had to worry about when you were younger.

Keep clean
You have sweat glands all over your skin. When you get hot, your body perspires to help cool you down. The perspiration is a mixture of water and salt and doesn't smell. At puberty, new sweat glands develop under the arms, around the nipples, navel, and in the inner lips of the vulva. These are scent glands, which give you your individual smell, but if you get too hot and sweaty, the smell becomes kind of stale or funky.

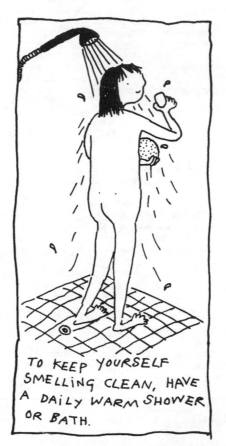

TO KEEP YOURSELF SMELLING CLEAN, HAVE A DAILY WARM SHOWER OR BATH.

To keep yourself smelling clean, take a warm bath or shower daily. Remember to wash well, especially under your arms and between your legs. Always wash your vulva and buttocks from front to back, so you don't infect your vagina with any of the germs from the anus. This also applies to wiping your behind after going to the bathroom—always go from front to back.

After a shower or bath, change into clean underpants. Cotton ones are best, because synthetic ones tend to keep in heat and moisture unless they have a cotton crotch.

You may want to start using an underarm deodorant or antiperspirant—particularly during a period when your sweat glands are more active. There are many natural and nonchemical products now on the market.

Keeping clean during a period

You may hear people say you shouldn't wash your hair or take a bath when you've got a period. Baloney!

It's quite OK to take a bath, as long as it's not too hot. The flow of blood usually slows while you're in warm water, but it doesn't stop completely. If you use tampons, you can leave one in while you're bathing, but put in a clean one afterward. If you use sanitary pads, make sure you have one handy for when you come out of the bath. Pat your vulva dry with tissues or toilet paper before you put it on. If your thighs become sore from wearing sanitary pads, dab talcum powder on your thighs.

Remember to change your pad or tampon regularly—three or four times a day, and maybe even more during the first few days. Menstrual blood begins to smell slightly when it reaches the air and the warmth of your body increases the smell.

If your underpants get blood on them, the best way to get rid of the stains is to soak and rub the fabric in cold, salty water before you wash them.

Take care of your skin

The hormones whizzing around your body make your skin glands particularly active. The extra oil

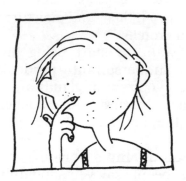

I HAVE REALLY BAD
SKIN AROUND THE
TIME OF MY PERIOD.

they produce can clog the pores and give you pimples on your face and sometimes your back and other parts of your body as well.

The simplest way to unclog pores is to wash your face morning and night with antibacterial soap and warm water. Then use an antiseptic liquid to tighten the pores. If your face is sensitive to soap, buy an antibacterial face lotion or cream from a pharmacist.

Some experts have suggested that people with pimples should avoid fatty and greasy foods, such as chocolate, fries, and cheese, and eat plenty of fresh fruit instead. Others think that foods have nothing to do with pimples. Experiment for yourself to see if there's a particular food that makes you break out. If so, avoid it!

It's very tempting to pick and squeeze pimples. Don't! It may only make them worse and can even cause permanent scarring! If all else fails, put a dab of drying agent on the worst ones, and try to forget about them.

CHOOSE A SHAMPOO FOR GREASY HAIR, GIVE YOUR HAIR ONLY ONE LATHERING AND MAKE SURE YOU RINSE ALL THE SHAMPOO OUT.

Care for your hair

My hair's gotten all greasy.

At puberty, the oil glands in your scalp that keep your hair healthy often start working overtime, making your hair greasy instead. Choose a shampoo for oily hair, give your hair only one lathering, and make sure you rinse all the shampoo out. Your hair should squeak when it's clean!

Sleep well

I seem to need more sleep than I used to.

You may find that your sleep pattern is changing. Your own rhythm is what suits you best—don't fight it or compare it with your friends. People need different amounts of sleep. You might need nine or ten hours a night, while a friend might need only seven or eight hours, or the other way around. If you find you're particularly tired during your period, get some extra sleep.

If you have problems getting to sleep, it may be that your body doesn't need as much sleep as you think. It's better to stay up or read in bed until you feel sleepy, rather than going to bed and worrying about not being able to get to sleep. You may find that a cup of chamomile tea or warm milk helps calm you down. If you can't get to sleep because you're worrying about a problem, try to share it with someone. Fresh air and exercise during the day will always help you sleep better.

Too much sleep, on the other hand, can make you feel just as bad as not enough. Don't stay in bed longer than you need, particularly if you have period cramps. It'll only make you feel worse.

Rest is just as important as sleep. Try to find half an hour or more every day to relax, however pressured you may feel. Lie flat on the floor and let your muscles relax one by one, or sit in a chair and concentrate on a spot on the wall. Go for a walk and concentrate on breathing, not on thinking, or lie on your bed with your eyes closed and listen to some relaxing music.

Shape up
There have been a number of sensationalistic stories in the newspapers about how out of shape teenagers are becoming. Don't let yourself be one

of them! Daily exercise, even if only ten minutes of stretching, will help your body stay in good shape. If you can do twenty minutes of aerobic exercise three times a week, even better. As well as keeping you physically fit, exercise may also help menstrual cramps.

Tennis, swimming, softball—there are many exercise options. But if organized sports aren't locally available or aren't your idea of fun, there are plenty of other ways to keep in shape. Run up and down the stairs five times a day; take the dog for a long walk every morning; dance to your favorite music; go for a bicycle ride with a friend, or go roller blading.

You can tone some of your muscles even while you're sitting down. Clench your buttocks and thigh muscles; press your feet into the floor; circle your arms around and around; swing your head gently in a circle, first one way and then the other.

Whatever exercise you choose to do, try to do it regularly. Don't find an excuse to quit. If you start to find it boring, try exercising with a friend or in time to music. If you exercise at the same time every day, say when you get up, it will become as much of a habit as brushing your teeth or washing your face.

An exercise routine

If you do get menstrual cramps or backaches, then it's a good idea to do extra exercises to loosen and relax you. The following exercises are designed to strengthen your tummy and pelvic muscles and should help relieve cramps. You might not notice any difference for the first month or so, but if you do the exercises regularly, they should start being effective.

Exercise 1

Repeat ten times.

Stand up straight with your feet apart and your arms stretched out at shoulder height.

Keeping your arms straight, swing your right hand down to touch your left foot. Come back to your starting position.

Then swing your left hand down to touch your right foot.

Exercise 2

Repeat ten times.

Stand in the same starting position as for Exercise 1.

Twist your body and right arm to the left, without moving your feet. Keep both arms straight and at shoulder height. Return to the starting position, and then twist your body and left arm to the right.

Exercise 3

Repeat ten times.

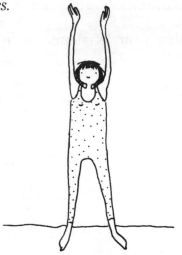

Stand with your feet apart and your arms stretched straight above your head.

Keeping your knees straight, bend down and touch your toes. Return to the starting position with your arms still at full stretch.

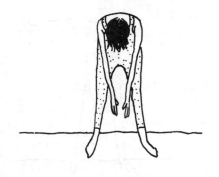

Exercise 4

Repeat ten times.

Sit on the floor with your legs and feet together and your knees straight. Put your hands on your shoulders.

Stretch forward and put your fingers on your toes (if you can't reach them at first, bend your knees).

Return to the starting position.

Exercise 5

Repeat five times.

Kneel with your hands flat on the floor. Breathe in slowly. As you breathe out, arch your back, pull in your tummy muscles, and look down toward your knees.

Now breathe in. As you do so, lift your head upward and flatten your back at the same time. Keep your arms straight the entire time.

Exercise 6

Sit on your heels with your arms in front of you. Gradually stretch forward until your tummy is stretched right over your legs, your forehead is touching the floor, and your arms are stretched as far as they will go. Relax and breathe deeply.

ENJOY EATING

Enjoy eating
In the year before your period starts, it's very likely that you'll put on about eleven pounds. In the following two years, you may put on another seven to twelve pounds a year until you reach your adult weight. This weight gain is absolutely normal. It does *not* mean you're going to end up fat. You'll be growing taller and your limbs will be growing longer at the same time.

You need to eat enough to grow properly and to give you energy for everything you do. Some girls worry so much about their weight that they starve themselves (*anorexics*) or stuff themselves and then throw up (*bulimics*). Strict diets and crash diets aren't a good idea when you're growing, as they can permanently harm your body and upset your menstrual cycle.

If you want to keep yourself in shape, just remember these three things: Eat plenty of fresh fruit and vegetables; limit sugary and high fat foods like chocolate, candy, and cookies; and exercise regularly.

Chapter 7

What If . . . ?

(Questions about periods)

Having your period should be as simple as eating, sleeping, or going to the bathroom, but sometimes people worry about it. If you think you have a problem, share it with someone, don't keep it to yourself. The sooner someone can help you, the less time you'll spend worrying.

What if I have vaginal discharge?

You're likely to have vaginal discharge before a period and also when you ovulate (midway between periods). A normal vaginal discharge is a small amount of white or colorless fluid.

But if your discharge changes in any of the following ways, tell someone close to you or go see a doctor:

➦ If it becomes discolored (yellow or blood-stained) and smelly. First check that you haven't left a tampon in.

➦ If it becomes much thicker and heavier.

➦ If you get a constant sore, burning, or itching feeling.

A doctor can quickly tell whether a discharge is normal or not. You may have nothing wrong at all. Or, you may have a common infection called a *yeast infection*, which can be easily treated.

What if my period hasn't started yet?

If you haven't started your period yet and most of your friends have, don't worry. It doesn't mean you won't. It just means your body's timetable is different from theirs. Doctors call the absence of a period *amenorrhea*, pronounced a-men-or-EE-a. Sometimes girls don't start until they're sixteen or seventeen. But in the end, almost everyone does, just like these two girls eventually did.

I started developing early, with the exception of my period. My mom told me all about it when I was ten and gave me some sanitary pads to put away until I needed them—but nothing happened. I had my first bra, but still no period. I wondered if I was normal. The longer I waited, the more I worried about what could be wrong. At first, only a few of my friends started, then almost all of them did. Everyone assumed I'd started, so I couldn't confide in anyone.

My mom told me not to worry, so did the doctor. But I wanted proof! Every time I had something like a stomachache, I thought my period was starting, but it never did. I had all sorts of fantasies about what was wrong. The doctor couldn't find anything wrong at all. When I was fifteen, she told me to wait another six months and eat plenty of oranges (for vitamin C). Finally, three months later, I had my first period. What an anticlimax! I was nearly sixteen!

◆ ◆ ◆

My period didn't begin until I was past seventeen. As far as my friends were concerned, I'd started three years before, when most of them began theirs. For three years I'd lived this lie, because I didn't want them to laugh at me for being a late starter. I couldn't think why I didn't have periods like them. I kept quiet about it for years.

Then I noticed that every so often my friends would ask to be excused from swimming and showers after games. Ah ha! So every once in a while I'd do the same. The times I chose to be excused, I'd also make a point of complaining of a stomachache and all the other things my friends seemed to do.

Unfortunately for me, we had a P.E. teacher who kept a log of who was excused from showers and when. She mentioned to the school doctor, on a check-up visit, that my period was totally irregular. I was caught. I had to admit that it was all a fib. I felt better, though, having told someone. It was not long after this that my period actually started. Once I'd started and saw what was involved, I wondered why I'd been so anxious to start in the first place!

What if my period is heavy?

Although the flow may look only like blood, in fact blood makes up only half of it. The rest includes the remains of the extra lining of the uterus and sticky mucus from the cervix and vagina.

The amount of blood you lose is actually very little—the equivalent of between four and eight tablespoons—even if it looks like a lot more.

The amount of blood there is varies from person to person and month to month. If there's a lot of blood, that's just as healthy as not very much. Your body soon replaces whatever blood you lose.

Periods are considered heavy if:

•✦ You *need* (instead of *choose*) to use more than six pads or tampons a day, every day of your period.

•✦ Your period lasts for much more than a week.

•✦ You have more than one period a month and you feel tired and sleepy, even though you're eating well and sleeping normally.

Heavy periods can be caused by shock or worry or upset to your normal routine, such as changing schools, going on vacation, and so on. On the other hand, they could mean that your uterus is not working quite the way it should. If your period suddenly becomes heavier and you can't think of a good reason, it is a good idea to see a doctor.

The doctor might suggest that you eat extra amounts of some iron-rich foods, such as brown bread, liver, raisins, or watercress, or might prescribe iron tablets.

What if my period comes late or skips a month?

More often than not, for the first two years or so, your periods may be irregular. This is because you haven't started ovulating (see page 46). Hormones send messages to make the lining of your uterus thicken, but the messages are often erratic.

As your ovaries mature, you'll begin ovulating—not necessarily every month at first, maybe every two or three. Once you ovulate regularly every month or so, you should notice a more definite pattern to your cycle, and your period will probably become heavier.

Lots of things can upset your cycle, such as illness or an emotional upset, sudden changes, such as traveling, changing schools or living situations, hard physical work, exams, or an unhealthful diet.

Your period might stop completely for a while, or you may have lighter or heavier periods than usual. After a break, you might find that your cycle becomes longer or shorter than it was before.

Once you have a regular cycle, you only need to worry about irregular periods if:

➪ The pattern changes for no apparent reason and becomes much heavier or lighter.
➪ You miss two periods in a row—and there's no chance of your being pregnant—or if you miss one period and think you might be pregnant.

It's worth going to the doctor for a check-up about either of these.

What if I have bleeding between periods (called *spotting*)?

If you notice any bleeding between periods, you should always see a doctor about it, because it's not a usual thing to have happen. If it's only light spotting during the middle of the cycle, it probably has to do with ovulation. At this time, some people have a slight pain in either the right or left side of their tummy. This is a sign that the egg is leaving the ovary. However, if the pain lasts for more than a day or so, it might be a sign of illness, so it's worth going to see a doctor.

What if I feel faint during my period?

Occasionally, girls feel faint during their period. If this happens to you, go to bed early and avoid standing up for long stretches of time—sit down or walk around instead.

When you feel faint, sit down with your head between your knees until you feel better, and then have a drink of cold water. Or you could lie flat on the floor with your feet resting on a chair or your bent knees hugged toward your chest.

What if my breasts feel sore during a period?

Sore breasts are quite common before and during a period. It doesn't mean anything is wrong with them. Fluid builds up in them as a result of hormonal changes and may make them feel more tender. After the period, your breasts will go back to normal.

Before a period, my breasts get bigger and my nipples get sore. I even have to wear a bigger bra.

Usually for a week before my period my breasts feel very lumpy and tender.

These changes often go completely unnoticed. If they bother you, wear a slightly bigger bra and take a warm bath.

On the whole your breasts won't feel lumpy after a period. If they do, it may be normal, but you would be wise to see a doctor.

What if I get cramps and other pains?

Before you start ovulating, it's unlikely, though not impossible, that you'll have painful periods. Once ovulation happens regularly you might start having cramps and pains during your period, but not necessarily. In any case, people feel pain quite differently—what one person can handle may be unbearable to someone else.

Many people have discomfort rather than pains:

I get a draggy feeling, but it isn't bad pain. I feel constipated and have a feeling of fullness in the first few days of a period.

I can feel my uterus contract and tension builds up. My stomach feels heavy and aches.

Some people, however, have quite severe pains:

Usually on the first day, I have a lot of
pain and an upset stomach. I feel sick
(often bad enough to have to go to bed for
most of the day).

The pain usually has to do with your period, but not always. You might be constipated as well. If so, try to eat foods with plenty of fiber (such as brown bread, fruit, salads, and raw vegetables). Or it may be because you're worried about your period. Worry can make you feel tense and knotted up or even increase your discomfort. It may even be that you get pain because you're expecting it:

I often get bad cramps, but if I pretend I
haven't got them, they go away.

If you do get pain, don't just grit your teeth and stand it. There are plenty of things you can do to relieve it. On the next couple of pages are some people's suggestions. Try some of them out and see which work best for you.

If the pain is more than you can bear, go to your doctor and ask for advice. There are several medical ways of helping to lessen menstrual cramps.

I GO FOR A WALK, DRINK LOTS OF WATER AND HAVE SOME EARLY NIGHTS.

I MAKE SURE I EAT WELL TO KEEP UP MY ENERGY. I ALSO TAKE VITAMIN C.

I HUG A HOT-WATER BOTTLE AGAINST MY TUMMY. I TRY NOT TO MOVE AROUND TOO MUCH. SIT UP STRAIGHT INSTEAD OF SITTING IN MY USUAL SLOPPY WAY AND MAYBE TAKE A PAIN-KILLER.

IF I CAN I EXERCISE, WHICH ISN'T AT ALL GOOD AT FIRST, BUT IF I SURVIVE, THEN IT'S VERY GOOD!

I MASSAGE MY STOMACH AND BACK. I FIND IT HELPFUL TO PRESS AND RUB THE BOTTOM OF MY SPINE WITH MY KNUCKLES OR FINGERTIPS.

I TRY TO RELAX AND BREATHE DEEPLY.

USUALLY I LIE ON MY BACK WITH MY KNEES UP.

I TAKE A LONG BATH AND GO TO BED WITH A CUP OF TEA. SOMETIMES LYING ON MY TUMMY HELPS.

Chapter 8

Brochures and Samples

The following sources provide additional information regarding menstruation in the form of toll-free consumer information phone numbers, brochures, or product samples:

**Johnson and Johnson
Consumer Products, Inc.
Skillman, N.J. 08558
(800) 526-3967**

- Provides free pamphlets on the subjects of puberty and menstruation.

**Kimberly-Clark Corporation
Consumer Services
P.O. Box 2020
Neenah, WI 54957-2020
(800) 544-1847**

- Offers a kit: *Kotex® Becoming Aware®* $3.00. Kit includes *Parent's Guide, Sarah's Story* booklet, Kotex® product samples and coupon.

**Playtex Products Inc.
Consumer Affairs Dept.
P.O. Box 728
Paramus, NJ 07652**

- Provides free product samples and information booklet on parent-teen communication and subjects of puberty and menstruation.

**TamBrands
P.O. Box 271
Palmer, Mass. 01069
(800) 523-0014
Internet website:
http://www.troom.com**

- Provides free samples and booklet: *Time for Answers.* Offers a kit for parents for $6.95. Kit includes product samples, *Time for Answers* booklet, a guide to parent-teen communication, and a 30-minute video.

Food and Drug Administration, HFE–88
5600 Fishers Lane
Rockville, MD 20857

- Provides a brochure, *On the Teen Scene: A Balanced Look at the Menstrual Cycle*; request brochure FDA94–1215.

Chapter 9

Additional Reading on Health and Sex Education

Dr. Ruth Talks to Kids: Where You Came From, How Your Body Changes, and What Sex Is All About by Dr. Ruth Westheimer. Illustrated by Diane deGroat. Macmillan Publishing Company, Inc., 1993

Growing and Changing: A Handbook for Preteens
by Kathy McCoy, Ph.D., and Charles Wibbelsman, M.D.
The Body Press,
Price Stern Sloan, Inc., 1987

How Sex Works
by Elizabeth Fenwick and Richard Walker.
Dorling Kindersley Publishing Inc., 1994

It's a Girl Thing: How to Stay Healthy, Safe, and in Charge
by Mavis Jukes.
A Borzoi Book,
Alfred A. Knopf, Inc., 1996

The New Teenage Body Book
by Kathy McCoy, Ph.D., and Charles Wibbelsman, M.D.
Illustrated by Bob Stover.
The Body Press,
Price Stern Sloan, Inc., 1987

The What's Happening to My Body? Book for Girls
by Lynda Madaras with Area Madaras. Second Edition.
Newmarket Press, 1983, 1988

Recommended Fiction

Are You There, God? It's Me, Margaret
by Judy Blume.
Dell Publishing Co., Inc.,
Macmillan Children's Book Group,
1970, 1972, 1990

Forever
by Judy Blume.
Macmillan Children's
Book Group, 1975

Chapter 10

Free Brochures on Sexual Health Topics

National Institute of Allergy and
Infectious Diseases
Office of Communications
Building 31, Room 7A50
31 Center Drive, MSC 2520
Bethesda, MD 20892–2520

- Provides *Sexually Transmitted Diseases Fact Sheets* with the following titles:
Chlamydia, Herpes, Gonorrhea, Syphilis, Hepatitis, HIV/AIDS, Human Papilloma Virus and Genital Warts, Pelvic Inflammatory Disease,

Vaginal Infections, and *Other Important STDs.* Request *Sexually Transmitted Diseases Fact Sheets* to receive entire packet, or request specific titles.

**Food and Drug Administration, HFE–88
5600 Fishers Lane
Rockville, MD 20857**

• Provides information on the following subjects:
Toxic shock syndrome: *On the Teen Scene: TSS Reducing the Risk*; request FDA92-1196. Sexually transmitted diseases: *On the Teen Scene: Preventing STDs*; request FDA95-1210. Yeast infections: *On the Teen Scene: Yeast Infections*; request FDA96-1236.

Notes

_____

_____

_____

_____

_____

_____

_____

_____

_____

_____

_____

_____

_____

Notes

_____

_____

_____

_____

_____

_____

_____

_____

_____

_____

_____

_____

_____

Notes

_____

_____

_____

_____

_____

_____

_____

_____

_____

_____

_____

_____

_____

_____

Notes

_____

_____

_____

_____

_____

_____

_____

_____

_____

_____

_____

_____

_____

Notes

_____

_____

_____

_____

_____

_____

_____

_____

_____

_____

_____

_____